Dear Parents:

Congratulations! Your child is taking the first steps on an exciting journey. The destination? Independent reading!

STEP INTO READING® will help your child get there. The program offers five steps to reading success. Each step includes fun stories and colorful art or photographs. In addition to original fiction and books with favorite characters, there are Step into Reading Non-Fiction Readers, Phonics Readers and Boxed Sets, Sticker Readers, and Comic Readers—a complete literacy program with something to interest every child.

Learning to Read, Step by Step!

Ready to Read Preschool–Kindergarten
• big type and easy words • rhyme and rhythm • picture clues
For children who know the alphabet and are eager to begin reading.

Reading with Help Preschool–Grade 1
• basic vocabulary • short sentences • simple stories
For children who recognize familiar words and sound out new words with help.

Reading on Your Own Grades 1–3
• engaging characters • easy-to-follow plots • popular topics
For children who are ready to read on their own.

Reading Paragraphs Grades 2–3
• challenging vocabulary • short paragraphs • exciting stories
For newly independent readers who read simple sentences with confidence.

Ready for Chapters Grades 2–4
• chapters • longer paragraphs • full-color art
For children who want to take the plunge into chapter books but still like colorful pictures.

STEP INTO READING® is designed to give every child a successful reading experience. The grade levels are only guides; children will progress through the steps at their own speed, developing confidence in their reading. The F&P Text Level on the back cover serves as another tool to help you choose the right book for your child.

Remember, a lifetime love of reading starts with a single step!

To Gavi
—J.R.

Text copyright © 2022 by Jean Reagan
Cover art and interior illustrations copyright © 2022 by Lee Wildish

Step into Reading, Random House, and the Random House colophon are registered trademarks of Penguin Random House LLC.

Visit us on the Web!
StepIntoReading.com
rhcbooks.com

Educators and librarians, for a variety of teaching tools, visit us at RHTeachersLibrarians.com

Library of Congress Cataloging-in-Publication Data is available upon request.
ISBN 978-0-593-47914-8 (trade) — ISBN 978-0-593-47915-5 (lib. bdg.) —
ISBN 978-0-593-47916-2 (ebook)

Printed in the United States of America
10 9 8 7 6 5 4 3 2 1
First Edition

This book has been officially leveled by using the F&P Text Level Gradient™ Leveling System.

How to DO A SCIENCE EXPERIMENT

by Jean Reagan
illustrated by Lee Wildish

Random House 🏠 New York

At school today,

I learned

a science experiment!

I will teach you,
Grandma.

We will make lava.

Do not worry.

The lava is not real.

First, make a volcano
with clay.

Put a hole in the top.
Good job, Grandma!

Now we put in
some white powder.

Hmm, I forget.

Is it salt?

Add some
red food coloring.

Get ready, Grandma!

Here comes the lava!

Pour in the vinegar.

Nothing!

Hmm. Let's try again.

Maybe at school
we used sugar.
Add some more
red food coloring.

Get ready, Grandma!

Here comes the lava!

Pour in the vinegar.

Nothing!

Hmm. Let's try again.

Grandma,
what other white powder
do you have?

I remember now.

We used baking soda!

Add some more
red food coloring.

Get ready, Grandma!

This is it!

Here comes the lava!

Pour in the vinegar.

Lava, lava everywhere!

A happy, stinky mess.

Good job, Grandma!